# IS EVERYTHING CONNECTED?

Kevin Cunningham

## PUBLISHERS

2001 SW 31st Avenue
Hallandale, FL 33009
www.mitchelllane.com

## THINKING ALOUD

First Edition, 2020.
Author: Kevin Cunningham
Designer: Ed Morgan
Editor: Sharon F. Doorasamy

Series: Thinking Aloud
Title: Is Everything Connected? / by Kevin Cunningham

Hallandale, FL : Mitchell Lane Publishers, [2020]

Library bound ISBN: 9781680203417
eBook ISBN: 9781680203424

PHOTO CREDITS: Design Elements, freepik.com, p. 14 Jononmac46 CC-BY-SA-3.0, U.S. public domain

# Contents

Words in **bold** throughout can be found in the Glossary.

## CHAPTER ONE

# MOTHERSHIP CONNECTION

"One of the sayings in our country is **Ubuntu**, the essence of being human," said South African clergyman and Nobel Peace prize winner Desmond Tutu. "Ubuntu speaks particularly about the fact that you can't exist as a human being in isolation. It speaks about our interconnectedness. You can't be human all by yourself."

The Zulu people of southern Africa have a saying: "A person is a person through others." The Shona people, also of southern Africa, call it *unhu*. Some Kenyans practice a similar philosophy called *harambee*, a word that means "all together for one."

## TO THE RESCUE

A Tumbuka folktale tells a story of oneness. Masozi's mean older sister made her chase away birds from the rice field. The sister refused to give Masozi food. Masozi sang about her misery in the field. The birds enjoyed her song while eating the rice. Soon they provided Masozi with meals.

Different cultures practice *ubuntu* in their own ways. But in general it refers to a bond that connects all human beings. As Tutu explained, "It is to say, 'My humanity is inextricably bound up in yours.' We belong in a bundle of life."

> THE SAME SUBSTANCE COMPOSES US—THE TREE OVERHEAD, THE STONE BENEATH US, THE BIRD, THE BEAST, THE STAR—WE ARE ALL ONE, ALL MOVING TO THE SAME END.
>
> —*Mary Poppins*, by P. L. Travers

The idea that we all are part of a giant human family goes back to ancient times. Many religions preach some version of it.

In the last two centuries, scientific discoveries have also expanded our vision beyond human connections.

More and more we see the entire earth—even the entire universe—as one system. The astrophysicist Neil DeGrasse Tyson said, "We are chemically connected to all molecules on Earth. And we are atomically connected to all atoms in the universe."

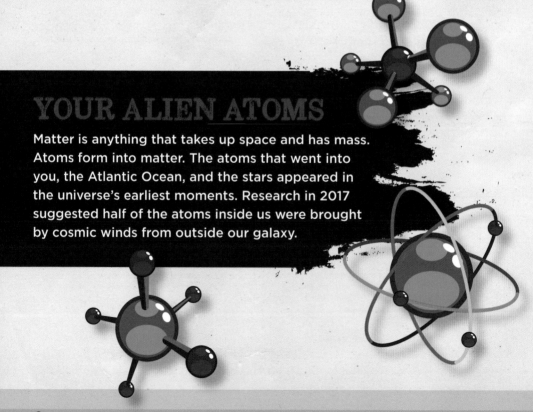

## YOUR ALIEN ATOMS

Matter is anything that takes up space and has mass. Atoms form into matter. The atoms that went into you, the Atlantic Ocean, and the stars appeared in the universe's earliest moments. Research in 2017 suggested half of the atoms inside us were brought by cosmic winds from outside our galaxy.

Philosophers have long looked at the world and asked: how does it all fit together? To find out, we must examine other questions. Can the need to solve global problems bring people together? Can anything? Is it possible a mathematical equation can explain the universe? The road to the answers stretches from prehistoric seas to beyond the stars.

## CHAPTER TWO

# In the Spirit

The idea of a **universal** connection among all people or even all living creatures came down to us from ancient times.

"Hinduism," said the Indian spiritual leader Mohandas Gandhi, "insists on the brotherhood not only of all mankind but of all that lives." The Hindu faith drew in part on texts called the Upanishads. Some of these ancient writings may date back to 800 BCE. The Upanishads spoke of a relationship among all people.

Mohandas Gandhi

> [PEOPLE] ARE BEGINNING TO AWAKEN TO AN IDEA: WE ARE ONE PEOPLE, ONE FAMILY, THE HUMAN FAMILY, AND WHAT AFFECTS ONE OF US AFFECTS US ALL.
>
> —Civil rights leader and politician John Lewis

Born in 643 CE, the Buddhist monk Fazang helped create a famed school of **Buddhism** in China. Huayen, or the Flower Garland School, centered on an idea called *shunyata*. As Fazang taught it, *shunyata* meant in part that everything in the universe shared a connection. But his philosophy went further. The universe included all things. All things caused all other things. All things influenced all other things.

## CONSPIRACIES EVERYWHERE

Some people insist NASA faked the 1969 moon landing. They say a famous movie director filmed the fakery and that all the NASA engineers and officials kept the secret. Believers dismiss proof like moon rocks as part of the plot. For such people, everything and everyone does connect . . . but only to the conspiracy.

Apollo 11 Lunar Module as it rested on lunar surface July 20, 1969.

In fact, the idea of universal **fellowship** appears in many religions. "Be devoted to one another in brotherly love," urged Paul, one of Christianity's early thinkers. As the Baha'i leader 'Abdu'l-Baha (1844–1921) put it, "There is perfect brotherhood underlying humanity." The Cree Indians built a belief system around *wahkohtowin,* or being related to all. Cree peoples in Canada still draw upon *wahkohtowin* in their laws and communities.

A Cree Indian in 1903

The idea of universal oneness influenced many philosophers. Baruch Spinoza suggested something called the **infinite** substance kept the universe bound together. The German philosopher Arthur Schopenhauer took Spinoza's idea and called it "will." He believed will controlled not just human actions but all of nature.

Some people think of religion and science as separate. Yet both explore the idea of being connected. Even in Schopenhauer's lifetime, scientists made discoveries that reinforced our sense of connectedness. The twentieth century, and the twenty-first, revealed how much we share with one another.

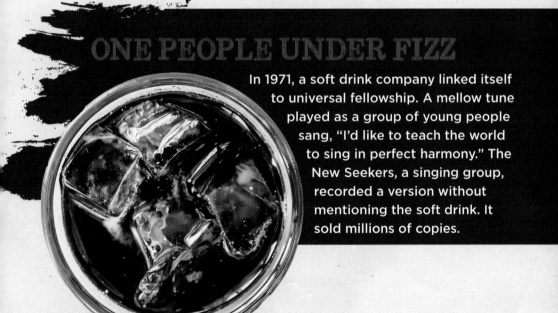

## ONE PEOPLE UNDER FIZZ

In 1971, a soft drink company linked itself to universal fellowship. A mellow tune played as a group of young people sang, "I'd like to teach the world to sing in perfect harmony." The New Seekers, a singing group, recorded a version without mentioning the soft drink. It sold millions of copies.

## CHAPTER THREE

# The Science of Everyone

Charles Darwin's ideas changed science. But the British thinker did far more. He led people to see the world in a new way. Darwin discussed how one form of life branched out, or evolved, into other forms. By changing very slowly over time, these prehistoric ancestors evolved into the creatures we know today.

Darwin famously said, "Probably all the organic beings which have ever lived on this earth have descended from one **primordial** form, in which life was first breathed."

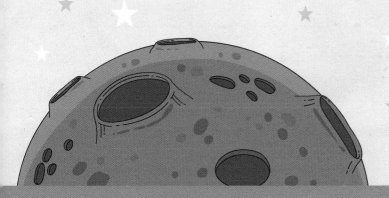

Tests on **DNA** have since revealed that Darwin was right. We are related to other life forms, sometimes in surprising ways.

Your DNA matches 99.9 percent of the DNA of the person next to you. That's true whoever is next to you. We share 96 percent with our fellow ape, the chimpanzee. But we're close to non-apes, too. Cows and humans carry about 80 percent of each other's DNA. For insects like fruit flies and birds like chickens, it's more than half—around 60 percent. We even share inactive DNA with plants.

Today's thinkers call "the one primordial form" LUCA. The term stands for "last universal common ancestor." That is, the last ancestor that all living things have in common. Imagine using a chart to trace back the ancestors of every animal and plant on earth. All the lines would meet at LUCA between 2 and 4 billion years ago.

The lines would also branch sideways. In 2010, a team of scientists made a blockbuster discovery. Many humans today carry DNA from Neanderthals.

Gibraltar skull

# YOU CAN'T PRESENT GOOD EVIDENCE THAT SAYS EVOLUTION IS NOT A FACT.

—Bill Nye

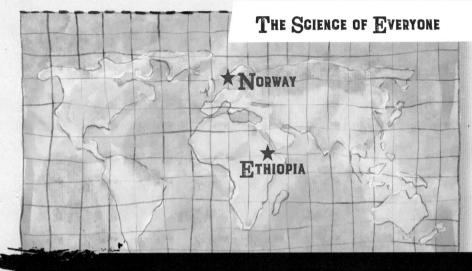

# WHAT DNA TELLS US

Many of us think of a Norwegian and an Ethiopian as belonging to totally separate races. Not so, says gene scientist Adam Rutherford. "If you take someone from Ethiopia and someone from the Sudan, they are *more* likely to be more genetically different from each other than either one of those people is to anyone else on the planet."

These prehistoric hunting people shared more than 99 percent of DNA with their non-Neanderthal human neighbors. Individuals from each species could, and did, have children together. The same thing happened with humans and Denisovans, a still-mysterious prehistoric people. Then, in 2018, scientists discovered Denisovans and Neanderthals had children, too. Future research may expand our list of relatives in other unexpected directions.

## CHAPTER FOUR

# THE SCIENCE OF EVERYTHING

rthur Tansley (1871–1955) coined the term **ecosystem** in the 1930s. The idea related to older thinking. American professor Aldo Leopold, for instance, had compared rivers, air, and other parts of the earth to organs in a living body. Tansley's idea reflected a belief that all living things **interact** with each other and their surroundings. He became famous for his work to conserve, or save, the environment. In 1950, King George VI knighted him.

Arthur Tansley in 1893

# DARWIN'S FAVORITE GAME?

In 1992, Maxis Software Inc. released *SimLife*. The video game allowed players to build an ecosystem. Players could make up their own life forms. They could also edit the DNA of plants and animals from the game. As time passed, new creatures evolved. The game tracked how well (or poorly) the ecosystem around them functioned.

"In nature, nothing exists alone," Rachel Carson (1907–1964) said. In her 1962 book *Silent Spring*, Carson showed how a human-made chemical called DDT damaged an ecosystem. A popular movement soon grew up around conserving the environment.

James Lovelock took the ecosystem idea further. His Gaia **hypothesis** mixed many fields of science with philosophy. Lovelock saw the earth as a huge system that took care of itself. Living and nonliving things, he said, worked together to encourage life.

Rachel Carson conducts marine biology research with Bob Hines in the Atlantic Ocean in December 1951.

Lynn Margulis, another scientist, added her expertise with microscopic life forms to expand Lovelock's hypothesis. Gaia, she said, was a "series of interacting ecosystems that compose a single huge ecosystem at the Earth's surface."

The Gaia hypothesis boosted interest in conservation. It encouraged new kinds of research. Many scientists, however, insisted it was wrong. Lovelock's ideas proved to have more power as philosophy—a way of seeing and explaining the world—than science.

'THE ANSWER TO THE GREAT QUESTION. . . . OF LIFE, THE UNIVERSE AND EVERYTHING. . . . IS. . . . FORTY-TWO,' SAID DEEP THOUGHT, WITH INFINITE MAJESTY AND CALM.

—*The Hitchhiker's Guide to the Galaxy*, by Douglas Adams

## EVOLUTION OF AN IDEA

Symbiosis refers to a relationship where two species depend on each other to live. Lynn Margulis studied a kind of symbiosis that explained how certain cells evolved. For years, other scientists refused to accept her findings. She kept insisting. Science now considers her work an essential part of biology.

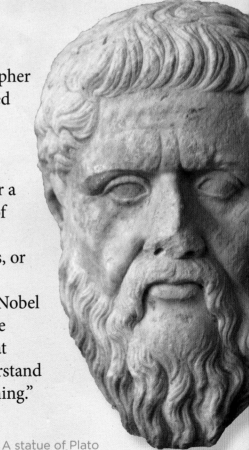

In *Timaeus*, the Greek philosopher Plato (c. 427-c. 347 BCE) proposed the universe is one system. Plato believed it operated according to mathematical rules.

Today's thinkers still search for a scientific explanation. A Theory of Everything would provide the mathematical equations that links, or unifies, all scientific knowledge. "Unification is where it's at," said Nobel Prize winner Steven Weinberg. He added, however: "I'm not sure that people are smart enough to understand whatever-it-is that unifies everything."

A statue of Plato

CHAPTER FIVE

# Oneness Songs, Oneness Stories

The arts bring people together. Humans probably gathered to drum and dance in prehistoric times. Plays filled outdoor theaters in ancient Greece while musicians and shadow puppet shows entertained the Chinese. For centuries, storytellers shared tales and poems with eager listeners in cultures around the world.

Today's entertainment does more than gather together a crowd for a good time. It brings messages of oneness and togetherness.

> # THE FORCE IS WHAT GIVES A JEDI HIS POWER. IT'S AN ENERGY FIELD CREATED BY ALL LIVING THINGS. IT SURROUNDS US AND PENETRATES US. IT BINDS THE GALAXY TOGETHER.
>
> —*Star Wars*, by George Lucas

Our shared connection has always inspired music. "One love, one heart," sang Jamaican superstar Bob Marley. "Let's get together and feel all right." French-Chilean hip hop artist Ana Tijoux uses music from around the world in her songs. Her hit "Somos Sur" featured Tijoux asking people to link arms to fight injustice. In the late 1960s, the idea of oneness made a splash in rock music with songs like "Get Together" by the Youngbloods.

## YOU CAN TUNA PIANO

A Chilean song inspired classical pianist Frederic Rzewski to compose "The People United Will Never Be Defeated!" In 2015, Rzewski brought his music to the public by playing it at a fish market in Pittsburgh. "I didn't expect people to come who wanted to hear music," he said. "I expected people to come who wanted to buy fish."

The togetherness **theme** appears often in film. Characters in *The Lion King* sang about it in "Circle of Life." Mufasa, meanwhile, explained to Simba how life interconnects. The Force linked everything in the sprawling *Star Wars* universe. Classmates ignored or made fun of Auggie Pullman in *Wonder*. But his ability to forgive and keep moving forward brought many people together.

The Global Oneness Project uses film, photos, and writing to build bridges between people in different lands. The contributors have journeyed into the Tibetan kingdom of Mustang, among woman storytellers of the Kara people of Ethiopia, and show the lives of workers who cut turf for fuel in rural Ireland. The stories share experiences. The stories reveal how people thousands of miles apart seek the same things.

The news seems to show people further apart than ever. Yet the dream of human togetherness has never been more popular. Wise leaders still show us how to connect with others. The Internet allows instant communication with people around the world. Satellites beam live sporting events and news. Every day science shows us more evidence that differences in appearance mean next to nothing.

We've proven that each of us connects to all life, human and otherwise. We've proven that each of us connects to the matter of the universe. The next question is: what will we do with the knowledge?

## FAMILY TREES

Harvard professor Henry Louis Gates Jr. hosted a TV show where scientific tests revealed the ancestors of guests. The musician Questlove, for instance, learned he had ancestors on the last slave ship to dock in the United States. Gates also connected comedian Larry David to Senator Bernie Sanders—a man he had impersonated on TV.

23

# SIX DEGREES

Frigyes Karinthy published the short story "Chains" in 1929. Karinthy's characters believed that every person on earth was a part of a chain. For example, one link connects you to your teacher. Your teacher grew up with a person named Joan. (Two links.) Joan went to law school with Barack Obama. Just three links in a chain, then, connect you to a former president.

In the 1990s, college students used "degrees of separation" instead of links. (The term came from a popular movie.) Their jokey game challenged players to find a link to film star Kevin Bacon. "Six Degrees of Kevin Bacon" soon became popular. Many people needed fewer than six degrees of separation to reach the actor.

Playing the six-degrees game is a fun way to see your connection to the rest of the human race. Think of a person you don't know. They can be famous or not. Investigate how you connect to them. You can start by asking those around you if they've met any notable people. Use books, the Internet, and your own knowledge to make further connections. You may find your way to Kevin Bacon.

# Selling the Connection

Take a look at some advertisements. You can watch them on TV or YouTube. You can read them in magazines or online. Notice what companies do to make their products attractive. Images, words, and music can play a big part. Whatever gets into the ad has one job: to make you feel good about the product.

Your job: use advertising to sell the idea of fellowship. Come up with an advertisement. You choose what kind. Draw the ad like a comic strip. (People who make ads call this a storyboard.) Using basic shapes like stick people is fine. What images could make togetherness look like a must-have for people? What words would work? Music can take the place of writing or work with it. Label your drawing to show where specific images, words, and music appear.

# Hidden Connections

Nicole Persley grew up in Virginia. People often asked about her background based on her appearance. She wondered why. She believed she had only European DNA. As an adult, she learned she had an African American grandfather. "That was a bombshell revelation for me and my family," she told the *Washington Post*.

These days, people can buy a DNA test kit at the drugstore. Results from these kits have surprised millions of people like Persley. Write a paragraph on the story of your "roots," or your ancestors. Why do you assume what you do about your family tree? What would you do if the truth turned out to be something different? Would it affect how you feel about yourself? Would it affect how you feel about others who share your ancestry?

# LIFTING THE VEIL

In 1971, philosopher John Rawls laid out an experiment. He asked people to put themselves behind what he called the "veil of ignorance." A person behind the veil of ignorance knows nothing about herself or her real life. As Rawls explained, "No one knows his place in society." That includes their wealth, their race, their age, where and how they live, and whether they're male or female. Nor do they know their personal traits, "intelligence, strength, and the like," as Rawls put it. Nor do they know anything about science or any other field of knowledge.

Imagine you stand behind the veil of ignorance. You know absolutely nothing about yourself. You have an equal chance of returning to the world as anything—a shopkeeper in Syria, a tailor in Afghanistan, an oil worker in Nigeria, or a banker in Brazil. That being the case, what kind of world do you hope waits when you step from behind the veil? Don't think in terms of "I hope to return as X." Instead, consider you might return as anyone. What would you want from life, no matter what? Do you see how the experiment breaks down our differences? What do you think Rawls discovered when he tried the experiment on people?

# MISSING LINKS

Let's make up a game. We'll call it Missing Links. Write the words listed below at random spots on a sheet of paper, art app, white board, or other surface. Write your name in the center. Now draw lines to connect any two words. On the line, write how the ideas connect. Keep in mind there may be more than one connection.

**butterfly**
**LUCA**
**a celebrity or athlete**
**the Sun**
**Sacagawea**

Try it again with a list of your own words. Challenge yourself to find more than one kind of connection between two words. And challenge yourself again to connect a single word to several other words.

# TIMELINE

**Plato**
A philosopher in Athens, Greece who addressed ideas about the universe

**Fazang**
An important Buddhist thinker born in 643 CE

**Charles Darwin**
A nature scientist best known for his work on evolution

**'Abdu'l-Baha**
A Bahá'í leader who spoke about fellowship

**P. L. Travers**
The Australian-British author of the *Mary Poppins* books

**Rachel Carson**
A marine biologist known for writings that helped start the modern environmental movement

**Desmond Tutu**
A South African clergyman and Nobel Prize winner who discusses the Ubuntu philosophy

**Lynn Margulis**
An American scientist, Margulis added ideas to James Lovelock's Gaia hypothesis

**Bob Marley**
A Jamaican singer-songwriter remembered for his many songs about unity and love

**Neil DeGrasse Tyson**
An astrophysicist famous for his talks on science

# GLOSSARY

**Buddhism**
A philosophy that looks for the nature of life and the universe

**DNA**
A material in almost all living things that determines their physical forms

**ecosystem**
A community of living things that interact with each other and their environment

**fellowship**
A close association with others, including strangers

**hypothesis**
An unproven idea proposed to explain something

**infinite**
Never ending

**interact**
To act against something else while also being acted upon by that thing

**primordial**
The era at the beginning of time

**theme**
 An idea or topic at the core of a story

**Ubuntu**
A philosophy that believes in a bond between all people

**universal**
Including all human beings, the entire world, or the entire universe

## FIND OUT MORE

Anders, Mason. *DNA, Genes, and Chromosomes*. North Mankato, MN: Capstone, 2017.

Lendler, Ian. *One Day a Dot: The Story of You, the Universe, and Everything*. New York: First Second Books, 2018.

Resler, T. J. *National Geographic Kids Guide to Genealogy*. Washington, DC: National Geographic Children's Books, 2018.

## WORKS CONSULTED

Astrobiology at NASA: Looking for LUCA, the Last Universal Common Ancestor
https://astrobiology.nasa.gov/news/looking-for-luca-the-last-universal-common-ancestor/

Britannica: Gaia Hypothesis
http://www.britannica.com/science/Gaia-hypothesis

Desmond Tutu Peace Foundation: Striving for Ubuntu
http://www.tutufoundationusa.org/2015/10/06/striving-for-ubuntu/

Stanford Encyclopedia of Philosophy: Original Position
https://plato.stanford.edu/entries/original-position/

## ON THE INTERNET

**Global Oneness Project**
https://www.globalonenessproject.org/

**National Women's History Museum: Rachel Carson**
https://www.womenshistory.org/education-resources/biographies/rachel-carson

**Smithsonian Institution: DNA: The Language of Life**
http://humanorigins.si.edu/evidence/genetics/ancient-dna-and-neanderthals/dna-language-life

**Templeton Prize: Who We Are (discussion with Desmond Tutu)**
https://www.youtube.com/watch?v=0wZtfqZ271w

**Worrall, Simon. "Why race is not a thing, according to genetics." National Geographic. October 14, 2017. Online.**
https://news.nationalgeographic.com/2017/10/genetics-history-race-neanderthal-rutherford/

# INDEX

# ABOUT THE AUTHOR

Kevin Cunningham is the author of more than 70 books for children and adults. One of his hobbies is asking big, impossible-to-answer questions. He lives near Chicago, Illinois.